should
go to the
orchestra!"

Not so fast!" said the entire orchestra in unison. "The Conductor didn't work alone. All of us have butchered a composer at one time or another. But we also keep composers alive. Without strings and woodwinds, without brass and percussion, there would be no composing at all. . . .

"Um, except for various kinds of nonorchestral music.

"If you want to hear the work of the world's greatest composers, you're going to have to allow for a little murder here and there."

"But—but that's injustice!" cried the Inspector.

"Those who want justice," said the orchestra, "can go to the police. But those who want something a little more interesting . . .

"Dead composers litter the musical world, and it's all because of one man . . . and one little stick! Arrest him at once!"

Mendelssohn!

Scriabin!

Liszt!

Messiaen!

Copland!

Cage!

Dvorak!

Shostakovich!

Ligeti!

Lutoslawski!

Corelli!

Bellini!

Puccini!

Rossini!

Scarlatti!

Busoni!

Boccherini!

Verdi!

J. C. Bach!

W. F. Bach!

C. P. E. Bach!

Offenbach! . . .

"Beethoven—dead!

Bach—dead!

Brahms—dead!

Mozart—dead!

Haydn—dead!

Schubert—unfinished, but dead!

Mahler—dead!

Chopin—romantic . . . but dead!

Tchaikovsky—dramatic . . . dead!

Stravinsky—ecstatic . . . dead!

Schoenberg—incomprehensible

. . . but dead!

Berlioz—dead.

Purcell—dead.

Prokofiev—dead.

Debussy—dead.

Vivaldi!

Wagner!

Sibelius!

Ives!

Handel!

Britten!

A strange noise caught the Inspector's ear.

"Of course," he said, "the Conductor! You've been murdering composers for years! In fact, wherever there's a conductor, you're sure to find a dead composer!

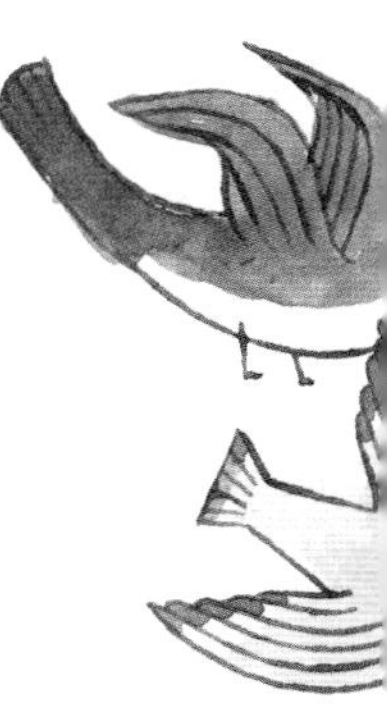

"The Violins waltzed.

"The Cellos and Basses provided accompaniment.

"The Violas mourned their fate, while the Concertmaster showed off.

"The Flutes did bird imitations . . . repeatedly, and the reed instruments had the good taste to admire my jacket.

"The Trumpets held a parade in honor of our great nation, while the French Horns waxed nostalgic about something or other.

"The Trombones had too much to drink.

"The Percussion beat the band, and the Tuba stayed home playing cards with his landlady, the Harp, taking sips of warm milk from a little blue cup.

"But the Composer is still dead."

pp
mp
MOZART
J.S.BACH

No," the Tuba said. "I'm a confirmed bachelor. I was home all night playing cards with my landlady, the Harp, taking sips of warm milk from a little blue cup."

The Inspector flipped through the pages of his notebook and scratched his handsome head with a well-manicured hand. "I'm utterly baffled," he said. "I've questioned all of the instruments in the orchestra, and none of them seems to be the murderer."

"And what about you, Tuba?" the Inspector said. "Were you involved in these distasteful shenanigans?"

"We were there, too," said the percussion instruments, barging in as only percussion instruments can do. "We drummed. We percussed. We employed xylophoniness and cymbalism. We heard the beat and beat the herd. We struck up and got down. We conquered the concert, battered the band, agitated the audience, rattled the roof, and got the phone numbers of several very attractive young sailors.

"By then we were beat—too exhausted to commit murder."

mf
mp
mf

Leave the French Horns alone," the Trombones said. "They were in such a state that we took them out to the club to cheer them up. We ordered a few bottles of expensive wine and then took the stage, swinging and dancing until dawn."

AHA! the Inspector cried, making a note in his notebook. "Perhaps you murdered the Composer for making you play so loud."

"We love being loud," the Trumpets replied. "Brass instruments are brassy by nature. Besides, loud is patriotic, and we suspect the murder was committed by a foreigner."

"A foreigner," the Inspector repeated. "What say you, French Horns? You have a strange accent."

The French Horns did not understand the question, and began murmuring a story about the Old Country.

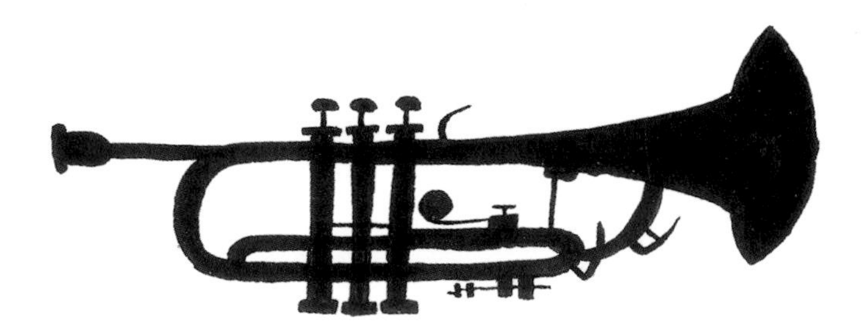

Last night was incredibly important for us," proclaimed the Trumpets in a boisterous manner, a phrase which here means "loudly and with a certain arrogant rudeness."

"We announced the arrival of Kings and Presidents. We led soldiers into battle and held a parade when they got home. Our ears are still ringing from all the ruckus."

“Ignore them,” said the First Oboe, leaning in close. “If I were you, I’d question the brass instruments instead. They’re a violent lot.”

“The brass?” the Inspector said, writing in his notebook. “You really think so?”

“You can trust me,” the Oboe said. “Everyone trusts me. After all, I tune up the entire orchestra by playing an A.”

“You can’t argue with that,” the Inspector said. “Brass, what do you have to say for yourselves?”

"Sneaky?" said the Clarinets. "We're not sneaky. By the way, Inspector, that's a very handsome jacket you are wearing."

"Oh—thank you," said the Inspector.

"Such shiny buttons," said the Bassoons.

"You think so?" the Inspector said, blushing slightly.

"And the color is very flattering," said the Oboes.

"Really?" the Inspector said, twirling around. "That's very kind of you to say so. But why are you giggling, Flutes?"

"Don't make us laugh!" the Flutes cried.
"We're much too wimpy and high-pitched for murder!
Ask the reed instruments—they're much sneakier than us."

"We were doing bird imitations," said the Flutes, the shiniest and highest pitched of the woodwinds. "It seems like that's all we ever do. Whenever the orchestra needs a bird, there we are."

AHA!

the Inspector cried. "Perhaps you murdered the Composer for making you act like birds!"

"You all have very good alibis," the Inspector said, taking notes in his notebook, "but the Composer is still dead.

"Perhaps the murderer is lurking in the woodwinds! Where were you last night, woodwinds?"

Everyone forgets about us," said the Violas bitterly. "We play the notes in the chords that nobody cares about. We play crucial countermelodies nobody hears. We often have to stay late after performances and stack up all of the chairs. We spent last night feeling sorry for ourselves as usual.

"But we did notice that the Concertmaster was acting strange. She was talking and laughing with the Composer, and carrying a strange black case."

The Concertmaster is the best violin player in the entire orchestra, and is often accused of treachery. "I was talking with the Composer about my cadenza," she said, using a word which here means "fancy solo part." "I'd never murder someone who was giving me such an excellent opportunity to show off."

AHA! the Inspector cried. "Perhaps you murdered the Composer for giving you such boring things to play!"

"On the contrary," the Cellos and Basses said. "We don't feel the need to show off like certain stringed instruments we could mention."

"Well, I guess that takes care of the strings," the Inspector said. "Oh—the Violas! I forgot all about you."

The Cellos and Basses sighed. The Cellos and Basses are often weary from dragging their large bodies around. The Basses in particular are so enormous that they can't even fit into taxicabs without sticking their curly heads out of the window.

"We were providing accompaniment," they said. "You can't waltz without a reliable one-two-three, one-two-three. It's boring, but it's steady work."

AHA! the Inspector cried, making a note in his notebook. "Perhaps you murdered the Composer for making you play so much."

"Don't be ridiculous!" the Violins said. "Violins are the stars of any orchestra. If we killed the Composer, we would have to find work at square dances or in romantic restaurants."

"That's true," the Inspector admitted. "But what about you, Cellos and Basses?"

"We were performing a waltz," said the Violins.
"We played graceful melodies so the ladies and
gentlemen could spin around and around and
around until they felt dizzy and somewhat
nauseous. This kept us busy all night."

The Violins answered first, of course. The violin section is divided into the First Violins, who have the trickier parts to play, and the Second Violins, who are more fun at parties.

The Inspector was a very handsome and intelligent person, not unlike myself. "I swear on my own intelligence and good looks," the Inspector said, "I will solve this terrible crime against humanity and/or classical music." And with an intelligent if somewhat flamboyant gesture, he reached into his pocket and took out the notebook he used for all official business. "First, I will interrogate the strings!" he cried. "Strings, where were you on the night in question?"

"I will find them if they are lurking in the strings.
"I will find them if they are lurking in the brass.
"I will find them if they are lurking in the woodwinds.
"I will find them if they are lurking in the percussion section.
"I will find them wherever they are lurking. I will find them!"

The Composer's death was very suspicious, and so the Inspector was called in to find the murderer or murderers and haul them off to jail.

"I will begin by interviewing all the usual suspects," the Inspector said. "Like all people in his line of work, this Composer had many enemies lurking in the orchestra. They can lurk all they like, but I will find them wherever they are lurking.

This is called decomposing.

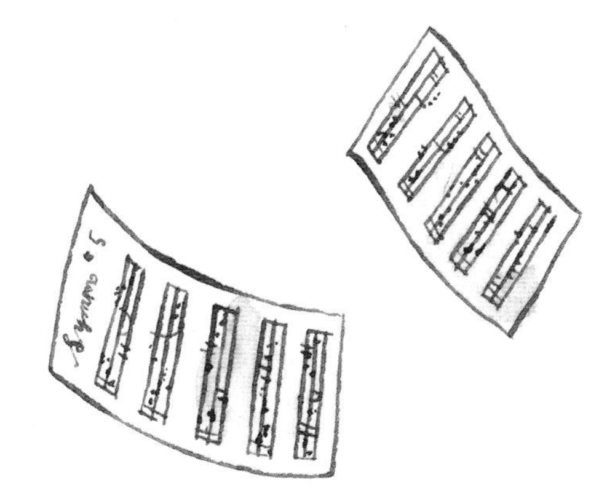

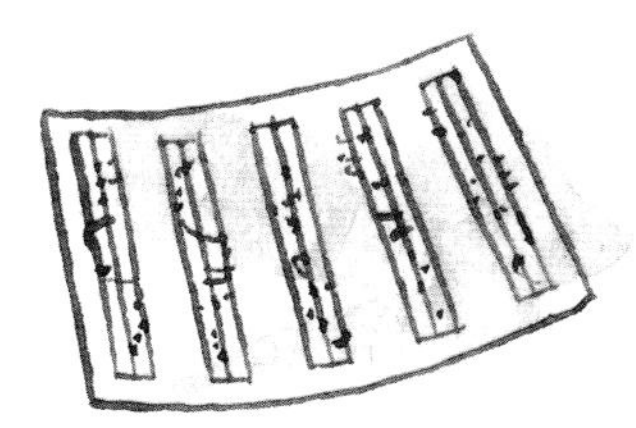

THE COMPOSER IS DEAD.

"Composer" is a word which here means "a person who sits in a room, muttering and humming and figuring out what notes the orchestra is going to play." This is called composing. But last night, the Composer was not muttering. He was not humming. He was not moving, or even breathing.

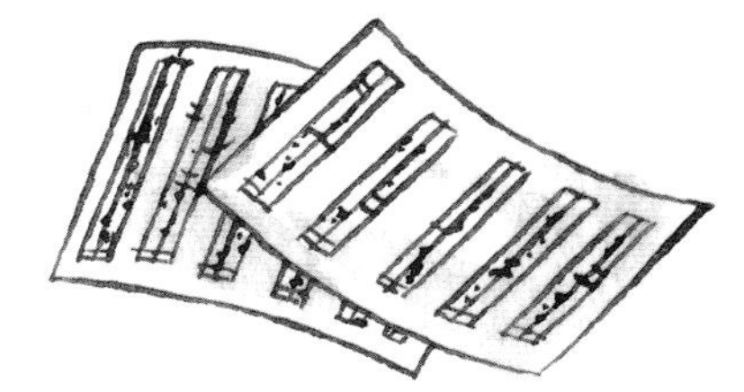

T

The Composer Is Dead

Manufactured in China.

For information address HarperCollins Children's Books, a division of HarperCollins Publishers, 1350 Avenue of the Americas, New York, NY 10019. www.harpercollinschildrens.com

Library of Congress Cataloging-in-Publication Data is available. Catalog card number: 2007020834
ISBN 978-0-06-123627-3 (trade bdg.) — ISBN 978-0-06-123628-0 (lib. bdg.)

Book design by Alison Donalty
1 3 5 7 9 10 8 6 4 2 ❖ First Edition